Contents

Dramatis Personæ 4

A Christmas Carol

Stave One
Marley's Ghost...7

Stave Two
The First of the Three Spirits 42

Stave Three
The Second of the Three Spirits........69

Stave Four
The Last of the Spirits.........................95

Stave Five
The End of it...127

What the Dickens? 144
The Dickens Family Tree.....................149
Dickens Timeline 150
Hard Times...152
A Very Victorian Christmas 154
Page Creation 156

Dramatis Personæ

Ebenezer Scrooge

Ghost of Jacob Marley

Ghost of Christmas Past

Ghost of Christmas Present

Ghost of Christmas Yet to Come

Bob Cratchit
Scrooge's clerk

Mrs. Cratchit
Bob's wife

Martha Cratchit
Bob's eldest daughter

Peter Cratchit
Bob's eldest son

Belinda Cratchit
Bob's second daughter

Cratchit children

Tiny Tim Cratchit
Bob's youngest son

Fan
Scrooge's sister

Schoolmaster

Mr. and Mrs. Fezziwig

Dick Wilkins
Scrooge's fellow apprentice

Belle
As a girl

Belle
As a married woman

Belle's husband

Fred
Scrooge's nephew

Alice
Fred's wife

Alice's sister

Topper
Friend of Fred

Ignorance and Want

Old Joe
Pawnbroker

Charwoman

Mrs. Dilber
Laundress

Undertaker

Caroline and her husband

A Christmas Carol

MARLEY WAS DEAD: TO BEGIN WITH. THERE IS NO DOUBT WHATEVER ABOUT THAT. THE REGISTER OF HIS BURIAL WAS SIGNED BY THE CLERGYMAN, THE CLERK, THE UNDERTAKER, AND THE CHIEF MOURNER.

OLD MARLEY WAS AS DEAD AS A DOOR-NAIL.

MIND! I DON'T MEAN TO SAY THAT I KNOW, OF MY OWN KNOWLEDGE, WHAT THERE IS PARTICULARLY DEAD ABOUT A DOOR-NAIL. BUT THE WISDOM OF OUR ANCESTORS IS IN THE SIMILE; AND MY UNHALLOWED HANDS SHALL NOT DISTURB IT, OR THE COUNTRY'S DONE FOR.

THERE IS NO DOUBT THAT MARLEY WAS DEAD.

THIS MUST BE DISTINCTLY UNDERSTOOD, OR NOTHING WONDERFUL CAN COME OF THE STORY I AM GOING TO RELATE.

SCROOGE AND HE WERE
PARTNERS FOR I DON'T
KNOW **HOW** MANY YEARS.

SCROOGE WAS HIS SOLE
EXECUTOR, HIS SOLE
ADMINISTRATOR, HIS
SOLE ASSIGN, HIS SOLE
RESIDUARY LEGATEE,
HIS SOLE FRIEND, AND
SOLE MOURNER. AND
EVEN SCROOGE WAS NOT
SO DREADFULLY CUT UP
BY THE SAD EVENT, BUT
THAT HE SOLEMNISED IT
WITH AN UNDOUBTED
BARGAIN.

SCROOGE NEVER
PAINTED OUT OLD
MARLEY'S NAME.

THERE IT STOOD, YEARS
AFTERWARDS, ABOVE
THE WAREHOUSE DOOR:

OH! BUT HE WAS A TIGHT-
FISTED HAND AT THE
GRINDSTONE, SCROOGE!

A SQUEEZING,
WRENCHING, GRASPING,
SCRAPING, CLUTCHING,
COVETOUS, OLD SINNER!

THE COLD WITHIN HIM
FROZE HIS OLD
FEATURES, NIPPED HIS
POINTED NOSE,
SHRIVELLED HIS CHEEK,
STIFFENED HIS GAIT;
MADE HIS EYES RED, HIS
THIN LIPS BLUE; AND
SPOKE OUT SHREWDLY IN
HIS GRATING VOICE.

EXTERNAL **HEAT** AND **COLD** HAD **LITTLE** INFLUENCE ON SCROOGE.

NO **WARMTH** COULD **WARM**, NOR **WINTRY WEATHER CHILL** HIM.

NOBODY **EVER** STOPPED HIM IN THE **STREET** TO SAY, WITH **GLADSOME LOOKS**, "MY DEAR **SCROOGE**, HOW **ARE** YOU? WHEN WILL YOU COME TO **SEE ME**?" NO **BEGGARS** IMPLORED HIM TO BESTOW A **TRIFLE**; NO **CHILDREN** ASKED HIM WHAT IT WAS **O'CLOCK**; NO **MAN** OR **WOMAN** EVER **ONCE** IN **ALL** HIS **LIFE** INQUIRED THE **WAY** TO **SUCH** AND **SUCH** A PLACE, OF **SCROOGE**.

EVEN THE **BLINDMEN'S DOGS** APPEARED TO KNOW HIM; AND WHEN THEY **SAW** HIM **COMING ON**, WOULD **TUG** THEIR **OWNERS** INTO **DOOR-WAYS** AND **UP COURTS**; AND THEN WOULD **WAG** THEIR **TAILS** AS THOUGH THEY SAID, "NO EYE AT **ALL** IS BETTER THAN AN **EVIL EYE**, DARK MASTER!"

BUT WHAT DID **SCROOGE** CARE! IT WAS THE **VERY THING** HE LIKED.

TO **EDGE** HIS **WAY** ALONG THE **CROWDED PATHS** OF LIFE, WARNING **ALL HUMAN SYMPATHY** TO **KEEP** ITS **DISTANCE**.

ONCE UPON A TIME - OF ALL THE GOOD DAYS IN THE YEAR, ON CHRISTMAS EVE - OLD SCROOGE SAT BUSY IN HIS COUNTING-HOUSE.

IT WAS A COLD, BLEAK, BITING WEATHER: AND HE COULD HEAR THE PEOPLE IN THE COURT OUTSIDE BEATING THEIR HANDS UPON THEIR BREASTS.

THE CITY CLOCKS HAD STRUCK THREE, BUT IT WAS QUITE DARK ALREADY.

THE **DOOR** OF SCROOGE'S **COUNTING-HOUSE** WAS **OPEN** THAT HE MIGHT KEEP AN **EYE** ON HIS **CLERK**; WHO IN A **DISMAL LITTLE CELL** BEYOND, WAS COPYING LETTERS.

SCROOGE HAD A **VERY SMALL FIRE**, BUT THE **CLERK'S** FIRE WAS SO **VERY** MUCH **SMALLER** THAT IT LOOKED LIKE **ONE COAL**. BUT HE COULDN'T **REPLENISH** IT, FOR SCROOGE KEPT THE **COAL-BOX** IN HIS **OWN** ROOM.

WHEREFORE THE **CLERK** TRIED TO **WARM HIMSELF** AT THE **CANDLE**;

IN WHICH **EFFORT**, **NOT** BEING A MAN OF **STRONG IMAGINATION**, HE **FAILED**.

13

15

There's another fellow, my *clerk*, with *fifteen shillings a-week*, and a *wife* and *family*, talking about a *Merry Christmas*.

I'll *retire* to Bedlam.

SCROOGE AND MARLEY'S, I BELIEVE. HAVE I THE PLEASURE OF ADDRESSING MR. SCROOGE; OR MR. MARLEY?

MR. MARLEY HAS BEEN DEAD THESE SEVEN YEARS. HE DIED SEVEN YEARS AGO; THIS VERY NIGHT.

WE HAVE NO **DOUBT** HIS **LIBERALITY** IS WELL REPRESENTED BY HIS **SURVIVING PARTNER**.

IT CERTAINLY **WAS**; FOR THEY HAD BEEN **TWO KINDRED SPIRITS**.

AT THIS **FESTIVE SEASON** OF THE **YEAR**, MR. **SCROOGE**, IT IS **MORE** THAN **USUALLY DESIRABLE** THAT WE SHOULD MAKE SOME SLIGHT **PROVISION** FOR THE **POOR** AND **DESTITUTE**, WHO SUFFER **GREATLY** AT THE **PRESENT TIME**.

MANY **THOUSANDS** ARE IN WANT OF COMMON **NECESSARIES**;

HUNDREDS OF THOUSANDS ARE IN WANT OF **COMMON COMFORTS**, SIR.

ARE THERE NO **PRISONS**?

PLENTY OF PRISONS.

AND THE **UNION WORKHOUSES**? ARE **THEY** STILL IN OPERATION?

THEY **ARE**. STILL, I WISH I COULD SAY THEY WERE **NOT**.

THE **TREADMILL** AND THE **POOR LAW** ARE IN **FULL VIGOUR**, THEN?

BOTH **VERY BUSY**, SIR.

OH! I WAS **AFRAID**, FROM WHAT YOU **SAID** AT **FIRST**, THAT **SOMETHING** HAD OCCURRED TO **STOP THEM** IN THEIR **USEFUL COURSE**. I'M **VERY GLAD** TO **HEAR IT**.

17

MANY **CAN'T** GO THERE; AND **MANY** WOULD RATHER **DIE**.

IF THEY WOULD RATHER **DIE**, THEY HAD BETTER **DO IT**, AND **DECREASE** THE **SURPLUS POPULATION**.

BESIDES --

-- EXCUSE ME --

-- **I** DON'T KNOW THAT.

BUT YOU **MIGHT KNOW** IT.

IT'S **NOT** MY **BUSINESS**. IT'S ENOUGH FOR A MAN TO UNDERSTAND HIS **OWN BUSINESS**, AND NOT TO **INTERFERE** WITH OTHER PEOPLE'S.

MINE OCCUPIES ME CONSTANTLY.

GOOD AFTERNOON, GENTLEMEN!

SCROOGE RESUMED HIS **LABOURS** WITH AN **IMPROVED OPINION** OF HIMSELF; AND IN A MORE **FACETIOUS TEMPER** THAN WAS **USUAL** WITH HIM.

THE COLD BECAME INTENSE. PIERCING, SEARCHING, BITING COLD.

GOD BLESS YOU MERRY GENTLEMAN! MAY NOTHING YOU DISMAY!

AT LENGTH THE *HOUR* OF *SHUTTING* UP THE COUNTING-HOUSE *ARRIVED*.

YOU'LL WANT **ALL DAY** TO-MORROW, I SUPPOSE?

IF QUITE **CONVENIENT,** SIR.

IT'S **NOT** CONVENIENT, AND IT'S **NOT FAIR.**

IF I WAS TO **STOP HALF-A-CROWN** FOR IT, YOU'D THINK YOURSELF **ILL-USED,** I'LL BE BOUND?

AND **YET,** YOU DON'T THINK **ME** ILL-USED, WHEN I PAY A **DAY'S WAGES** FOR **NO WORK.**

IT IS ONLY ONCE A YEAR, SIR.

A POOR EXCUSE FOR PICKING A MAN'S POCKET EVERY TWENTY-FIFTH OF DECEMBER!

BUT I SUPPOSE YOU MUST HAVE THE WHOLE DAY.

BE HERE ALL THE EARLIER NEXT MORNING!

THE CLERK PROMISED THAT HE WOULD; AND SCROOGE WALKED OUT WITH A GROWL.

THE CLERK WENT DOWN A SLIDE ON CORNHILL, AT THE END OF A LANE OF BOYS, TWENTY TIMES, IN HONOUR OF ITS BEING CHRISTMAS-EVE, AND THEN RAN HOME TO CAMDEN TOWN AS HARD AS HE COULD PELT, TO PLAY AT BLINDMAN'S-BUFF.

SCROOGE TOOK HIS *MELANCHOLY* DINNER IN HIS USUAL *MELANCHOLY TAVERN;*

AND HAVING **READ** ALL THE **NEWSPAPERS,** AND **BEGUILED** THE **REST** OF THE EVENING WITH HIS **BANKER'S-BOOK,** WENT **HOME** TO BED.

HE *LIVED* IN *CHAMBERS* WHICH HAD *ONCE* BELONGED TO HIS *DECEASED PARTNER.* IT WAS *OLD* ENOUGH NOW, AND *DREARY* ENOUGH, FOR *NOBODY* LIVED IN IT BUT *SCROOGE.*

SCROOGE HAD NOT BESTOWED *ONE THOUGHT* ON MARLEY, SINCE HIS *LAST* MENTION OF HIS *SEVEN-YEARS'* DEAD *PARTNER* THAT *AFTERNOON...*

23

THE STAIRCASE WAS BROAD...

IT WAS *PRETTY DARK*; SCROOGE DIDN'T CARE A *BUTTON* FOR THAT: *DARKNESS* IS *CHEAP*, AND SCROOGE *LIKED* IT.

SITTING ROOM, BED-ROOM, LUMBER-ROOM. ALL AS THEY *SHOULD* BE.

...WHICH IS *PERHAPS* WHY SCROOGE THOUGHT HE SAW A *LOCOMOTIVE HEARSE* GOING ON *BEFORE* HIM IN THE *GLOOM.*

QUITE *SATISFIED*, HE CLOSED HIS *DOOR*, AND *LOCKED* HIMSELF *IN*; *DOUBLE-LOCKED* HIMSELF IN, WHICH WAS *NOT* HIS *CUSTOM.*

HUMBUG!

HIS *GLANCE* HAPPENED TO REST UPON A *BELL*...

...A *DISUSED* BELL, THAT *HUNG* IN THE *ROOM*, AND *COMMUNICATED* FOR SOME PURPOSE NOW *FORGOTTEN* WITH A *CHAMBER* IN THE *HIGHEST STORY* OF THE *BUILDING*.

GDANG
GDANG
GDANG

THE BELLS *CEASED* AS THEY HAD *BEGUN,* TOGETHER.

27

SKRRCCH...

CREEAAAKK....

CLANK
CLANK
CLANK

IT'S HUMBUG STILL!
I WON'T BELIEVE IT.

CLANK
CLANK
CLANK

CLANK
CLANK
CLANK

I KNOW
HIM...

HOW NOW!
WHAT DO YOU **WANT**
WITH ME?

MUCH!

WHO **ARE**
YOU?

ASK ME
WHO I WAS.

MERCY!

DREADFUL APPARITION, WHY DO YOU TROUBLE ME?

MAN OF THE WORLDLY MIND!

DO YOU BELIEVE IN ME OR NOT?

I DO, I MUST. BUT WHY DO SPIRITS WALK THE EARTH, AND WHY DO THEY COME TO ME?

IT IS REQUIRED OF EVERY MAN, THAT THE SPIRIT WITHIN HIM SHOULD WALK ABROAD AMONG HIS FELLOW-MEN, AND TRAVEL FAR AND WIDE; AND IF THAT SPIRIT GOES NOT FORTH IN LIFE, IT IS CONDEMNED TO DO SO AFTER DEATH. IT IS DOOMED TO WANDER THROUGH THE WORLD --

-- OH, WOE IS ME! --

-- AND WITNESS WHAT IT CANNOT SHARE, BUT MIGHT HAVE SHARED ON EARTH, AND TURNED TO HAPPINESS!

OOOHHHHH AAAAHHH!

AAHHH!!

CLANK CLANK

RATTLE

33

YOU ARE FETTERED. TELL ME WHY?

I WEAR THE CHAIN I *FORGED* IN *LIFE.*

I *MADE* IT, *LINK* BY *LINK,* AND *YARD* BY *YARD;* I GIRDED IT ON OF MY OWN *FREE WILL,* AND OF MY OWN FREE WILL I *WORE* IT.

IS ITS *PATTERN STRANGE* TO YOU?

OR WOULD YOU *KNOW* THE *WEIGHT* AND *LENGTH* OF THE STRONG COIL YOU *BEAR YOURSELF?*

IT WAS FULL AS *HEAVY* AND AS *LONG* AS THIS, *SEVEN* CHRISTMAS EVES AGO.

YOU HAVE *LABOURED* ON IT, SINCE. IT IS A *PONDEROUS* CHAIN!

THERE *IS NO CHAIN* HERE!

34

"JACOB, OLD JACOB MARLEY, TELL ME *MORE*.

SPEAK *COMFORT* TO ME, JACOB!"

"I HAVE *NONE* TO GIVE."

"IT COMES FROM *OTHER* REGIONS, EBENEZER SCROOGE, AND IS *CONVEYED* BY *OTHER* MINISTERS, TO *OTHER* KINDS OF MEN."

"NOR CAN I *TELL* YOU WHAT I WOULD. A VERY *LITTLE* MORE IS ALL PERMITTED TO ME. I CANNOT *REST*; I CANNOT *STAY*; I CANNOT *LINGER* ANYWHERE."

"MY *SPIRIT* NEVER WALKED *BEYOND* OUR COUNTING-HOUSE --

-- *MARK ME!* --

-- IN LIFE MY *SPIRIT* NEVER *ROVED* BEYOND THE *NARROW* LIMITS OF OUR MONEY-CHANGING *HOLE*; AND WEARY JOURNEYS LIE BEFORE ME!"

"YOU MUST HAVE BEEN VERY *SLOW* ABOUT IT, JACOB."

"SLOW!"

"SEVEN YEARS *DEAD*.

AND *TRAVELLING* ALL THE TIME!"

"THE *WHOLE* TIME. NO REST, NO PEACE."

CLANK

CLANK

"INCESSANT *TORTURE* OF REMORSE!"

CLANK

AT *THIS* TIME OF THE ROLLING *YEAR*, I SUFFER *MOST*.

WHY DID I WALK THROUGH *CROWDS* OF *FELLOW-BEINGS* WITH MY EYES TURNED *DOWN*, AND NEVER *RAISE* THEM TO THAT *BLESSED STAR*, WHICH LED THE *WISE MEN* TO A *POOR ABODE*?

WERE THERE NO *POOR HOMES* TO WHICH ITS *LIGHT* WOULD HAVE *CONDUCTED ME*!

HEAR ME! MY *TIME* IS NEARLY *GONE.*

HOW IT IS THAT I APPEAR *BEFORE* YOU IN A *SHAPE* THAT YOU CAN *SEE*, I MAY NOT TELL.

I HAVE SAT *INVISIBLE BESIDE* YOU MANY AND MANY A DAY. THAT IS *NO LIGHT* PART OF MY *PENANCE*.

I WILL. BUT DON'T BE *HARD* UPON ME! DON'T BE *FLOWERY*, JACOB! *PRAY!*

I AM HERE TO-NIGHT TO *WARN* YOU, THAT YOU HAVE YET A *CHANCE* AND *HOPE* OF *ESCAPING* MY *FATE*. A CHANCE AND HOPE OF *MY PROCURING*, EBENEZER.

YOU WERE *ALWAYS A GOOD* FRIEND TO ME.

THANK'EE!

YOU WILL BE *HAUNTED*, BY *THREE SPIRITS*.

IS THAT THE *CHANCE* AND *HOPE* YOU MENTIONED, *JACOB?*

IT *IS*.

I - I *THINK* I'D RATHER *NOT*.

WITHOUT THEIR VISITS, YOU *CANNOT* HOPE TO *SHUN* THE PATH I TREAD. EXPECT THE *FIRST* TO-MORROW, WHEN THE BELL TOLLS *ONE*.

COULDN'T I TAKE 'EM *ALL* AT *ONCE*, AND HAVE IT *OVER*, JACOB?

EXPECT THE *SECOND* ON THE *NEXT NIGHT* AT THE *SAME HOUR*.

THE *THIRD* UPON THE *NEXT NIGHT* WHEN THE *LAST STROKE* OF *TWELVE* HAS CEASED TO *VIBRATE*.

LOOK TO SEE ME NO MORE; AND LOOK THAT, FOR YOUR *OWN SAKE*, YOU *REMEMBER* WHAT HAS *PASSED BETWEEN US!*

OOOOOHHHHH!

AAARGHHH!!

OOAAAAHH!!!

WHY, IT ISN'T *POSSIBLE.* THAT I CAN HAVE *SLEPT* THROUGH A *WHOLE DAY* AND *FAR* INTO *ANOTHER NIGHT.*

IT ISN'T *POSSIBLE* THAT ANYTHING HAS HAPPENED TO THE *SUN,* AND THIS IS *TWELVE* AT *NOON!*

THE *IDEA* BEING AN *ALARMING* ONE, HE *SCRAMBLED* OUT OF *BED* AND *GROPED* HIS WAY TO THE *WINDOW.*

ALL HE COULD *MAKE OUT* WAS, THAT IT WAS STILL *EXTREMELY COLD,* AND THAT THERE WAS *NO NOISE* OF *PEOPLE* RUNNING *TO* AND *FRO.*

WAS IT A *DREAM* OR *NOT?*

43

...UNTIL A MARKET-TOWN APPEARED IN THE DISTANCE.

These are but shadows of the things that have been.

They have no consciousness of us.

THEY LEFT THE HIGH-ROAD, BY A WELL REMEMBERED LANE, AND SOON APPROACHED A MANSION...

The school is not quite deserted. A solitary child, neglected by his friends, is left there still.

I... KNOW IT...

SCROOGE **WEPT** TO SEE HIS **POOR** FORGOTTEN SELF AS HE HAD **USED** TO **BE**.

54

IN THE **HALL** APPEARED THE **SCHOOLMASTER HIMSELF.**

BRING DOWN MASTER SCROOGE'S BOX, THERE!

HE THEN **CONVEYED** MASTER **SCROOGE** AND HIS **SISTER** INTO THE **VERIEST OLD PARLOUR,** WHILE THE **TRUNK** WAS **LOADED.**

GOOD-BYE, SIR!

55

Always a delicate creature, whom a breath might have withered.

But she had a large heart!

SO SHE **HAD**. YOU'RE **RIGHT**.

I WILL NOT **GAINSAY** IT, SPIRIT. GOD **FORBID**!

She died a woman, and had, as I think, children.

ONE CHILD.

True. Your nephew!

YES...

ALTHOUGH THEY HAD BUT *THAT MOMENT* LEFT THE *SCHOOL* BEHIND THEM...

...THEY WERE *NOW* IN THE BUSY *THOROUGHFARES* OF A CITY.

SAMUEL FEZZIWIG & Co.

Do you know this place?

KNOW IT! WAS I APPRENTICED HERE?

WHAT THEN? EVEN IF I HAVE GROWN SO MUCH WISER, WHAT THEN?

I AM NOT **CHANGED** TOWARDS **YOU**.

AM I? OUR CONTRACT IS AN **OLD** ONE.

IT WAS **MADE** WHEN WE WERE BOTH **POOR** AND **CONTENT** TO BE SO, **UNTIL**, IN **GOOD SEASON**, WE COULD **IMPROVE** OUR **WORLDLY FORTUNE** BY OUR **PATIENT INDUSTRY**.

YOU **ARE** CHANGED. WHEN IT WAS **MADE**, YOU WERE **ANOTHER MAN**.

I WAS A **BOY**.

YOUR **OWN** FEELING TELLS YOU THAT YOU **WERE NOT** WHAT YOU **ARE**.

I **AM**.

THAT WHICH PROMISED **HAPPINESS** WHEN WE WERE **ONE** IN **HEART**, IS **FRAUGHT** WITH **MISERY** NOW THAT WE ARE **TWO**. HOW **OFTEN** AND HOW **KEENLY** I HAVE **THOUGHT** OF THIS, I **WILL NOT SAY**.

IT IS **ENOUGH** THAT I HAVE **THOUGHT** OF IT, AND CAN **RELEASE** YOU.

63

THEY WERE IN *ANOTHER SCENE* AND *PLACE*. *NEAR* TO THE *WINTER FIRE* SAT A *BEAUTIFUL YOUNG GIRL*, SO LIKE THE *LAST* THAT *SCROOGE* BELIEVED IT WAS THE *SAME*, UNTIL HE SAW *HER*, SITTING BY *HER DAUGHTER*.

HA HA!

YAY!!

DADDY!!

BELLE, I SAW AN **OLD FRIEND** OF YOURS THIS **AFTERNOON.**

WHO **WAS** IT?

GUESS!

HA HA! HOW **CAN I?** ≈ TUT ≈ DON'T I **KNOW?**

-- MR. **SCROOGE.**

MR. SCROOGE IT **WAS!** I PASSED HIS **OFFICE WINDOW;** AND AS IT WAS NOT **SHUT UP,** AND HE HAD A **CANDLE** INSIDE, I COULD **SCARCELY HELP** SEEING HIM.

HIS **PARTNER** LIES UPON THE **POINT** OF **DEATH,** I HEAR; AND **THERE** HE SAT **ALONE.** QUITE **ALONE** IN THE **WORLD,** I **DO** BELIEVE.

SNOOOORE...

SNOOOR-UH!

DONG!

THE BELL WAS AGAIN UPON THE STROKE OF ONE.

SCROOGE FELT THAT HE WAS RESTORED TO CONSCIOUSNESS IN THE RIGHT NICK OF TIME; FOR THE ESPECIAL PURPOSE OF HOLDING A CONFERENCE WITH THE SECOND MESSENGER DESPATCHED TO HIM THROUGH JACOB MARLEY'S INTERVENTION.

71

HAVE NEVER WALKED FORTH WITH THE YOUNGER MEMBERS OF MY FAMILY; MEANING MY ELDER BROTHERS BORN IN THESE LATER YEARS?

I AM AFRAID I HAVE NOT.

HAVE YOU HAD MANY BROTHERS, SPIRIT?

MORE THAN EIGHTEEN HUNDRED.

A TREMENDOUS FAMILY TO PROVIDE FOR!

SPIRIT, CONDUCT ME WHERE YOU WILL.

I WENT FORTH LAST NIGHT ON COMPULSION, AND I LEARNT A LESSON WHICH IS WORKING NOW.

TO-NIGHT, IF YOU HAVE AUGHT TO TEACH ME, LET ME PROFIT BY IT.

TOUCH MY ROBE!

SPIRIT, I WONDER *YOU*, OF *ALL* THE *BEINGS* IN THE *MANY WORLDS* ABOUT US,

SHOULD *DESIRE* TO *CRAMP* THESE PEOPLE'S *OPPORTUNITIES* OF *INNOCENT ENJOYMENT*.

I!

YOU WOULD *DEPRIVE* THEM OF THEIR *MEANS* OF *DINING* EVERY *SEVENTH DAY*,

OFTEN THE *ONLY* DAY ON WHICH THEY CAN BE SAID TO *DINE* AT *ALL*.

WOULDN'T YOU?

I!

YOU SEEK TO *CLOSE* THESE PLACES ON THE *SEVENTH DAY*? AND IT *COMES* TO THE *SAME THING*.

I SEEK!

FORGIVE ME IF I AM **WRONG**. IT HAS BEEN **DONE** IN **YOUR NAME**, OR AT **LEAST** IN THAT OF YOUR **FAMILY**.

THERE ARE SOME UPON THIS **EARTH** OF YOURS, WHO LAY CLAIM TO **KNOW** US, AND WHO DO THEIR **DEEDS** OF PASSION, PRIDE, ILL-WILL, HATRED, ENVY, BIGOTRY, AND SELFISHNESS IN **OUR NAME**, WHO ARE AS STRANGE TO US AND ALL OUR **KITH** AND KIN, AS IF THEY HAD **NEVER LIVED**.

REMEMBER THAT, AND CHARGE THEIR **DOINGS** ON **THEMSELVES**, NOT US.

I WILL!

IT WAS A **REMARKABLE QUALITY** OF THE **GHOST** THAT **NOTWITHSTANDING** HIS **GIGANTIC** SIZE, HE COULD **ACCOMMODATE** HIMSELF TO **ANY PLACE** WITH **EASE**.

PERHAPS IT WAS THE **PLEASURE** THE **GOOD SPIRIT** HAD IN **SHOWING OFF** THIS **POWER** OF HIS, OR ELSE IT WAS HIS OWN **KIND, GENEROUS, HEARTY NATURE**, AND HIS **SYMPATHY** WITH ALL **POOR MEN**, THAT **LED** HIM **STRAIGHT** TO **SCROOGE'S CLERK'S DWELLING**.

76

...AND TREMBLED **MORE** WHEN HE SAID THAT *TINY TIM* WAS GROWING **STRONG** AND **HEARTY.**

AT **LAST** THE **DISHES** WERE SET ON; AND **GRACE** WAS SAID.

HURRAH!!

BANG!
BANG!
BANG!
BANG!
BANG!

IT WAS A **SUFFICIENT DINNER** FOR THE **WHOLE FAMILY.**

BUT **NOW,** THE **PLATES** BEING CHANGED BY MISS **BELINDA,** MRS. CRATCHIT **LEFT** THE ROOM **ALONE.**

OH! A WONDERFUL PUDDING!

THE **DINNER** WAS **ALL DONE,** THE **CLOTH CLEARED,** THE **HEARTH SWEPT,** AND THE **FIRE MADE UP.**

SCROOGE *HUNG* HIS
HEAD TO HEAR HIS
OWN WORDS QUOTED
BY THE *SPIRIT,* AND
WAS OVERCOME WITH
PENITENCE AND
GRIEF.

82

MAN, *IF MAN YOU BE* IN HEART, NOT ADAMANT, FORBEAR THAT *WICKED CANT* UNTIL YOU HAVE DISCOVERED WHAT THE SURPLUS IS, AND *WHERE* IT IS.

WILL *YOU DECIDE* WHAT MEN SHALL LIVE, WHAT MEN SHALL DIE?

IT MAY BE, THAT IN THE SIGHT OF HEAVEN, *YOU* ARE MORE WORTHLESS AND LESS FIT TO LIVE THAN MILLIONS LIKE THIS POOR MAN'S CHILD.

OH GOD!

TO HEAR THE INSECT ON THE LEAF PRONOUNCING ON THE *TOO MUCH LIFE* AMONG HIS HUNGRY BROTHERS IN THE DUST!

MR. SCROOGE!

I'LL GIVE YOU **MR. SCROOGE,** THE **FOUNDER** OF THE FEAST!

83

AS *SCROOGE* AND THE *SPIRIT* WENT ALONG THE *STREETS*, THE *BRIGHTNESS* OF THE ROARING *FIRES* IN KITCHENS, PARLOURS, AND ALL SORTS OF *ROOMS*, WAS *WONDERFUL*.

THE VERY *LAMP-LIGHTER*, WHO RAN *BEFORE* DOTTING THE *DUSKY STREET* WITH *SPECKS* OF *LIGHT LAUGHED* OUT *LOUDLY* AS THE SPIRIT *PASSED*.

BLESSINGS ON IT, HOW THE *GHOST EXULTED!*

MERRY CHRISTMAS!

MERRY CHRISTMAS!

AGAIN THE GHOST SPED ON...

...ON, ON - UNTIL BEING FAR AWAY FROM ANY SHORE...

...THEY LIGHTED ON A SHIP.

OH COME, ALL YE FAITHFUL, JOYFUL AND TRIUMPHANT...

IT WAS A GREAT SURPRISE TO SCROOGE TO HEAR A HEARTY LAUGH...

HA, HA! HA, HA, HA!

...IT WAS A MUCH GREATER SURPRISE TO SCROOGE TO RECOGNISE IT...

...AS HIS OWN NEPHEW'S.

HE SAID THAT CHRISTMAS WAS A HUMBUG, AS I LIVE! HE BELIEVED IT TOO!

MORE SHAME FOR HIM, FRED!

HE'S A COMICAL OLD FELLOW, THAT'S THE TRUTH: AND NOT SO PLEASANT AS HE MIGHT BE.

HOWEVER, HIS OFFENCES CARRY THEIR OWN PUNISHMENT; AND I HAVE NOTHING TO SAY AGAINST HIM.

I'M SURE HE IS VERY RICH, FRED. AT LEAST YOU ALWAYS TELL ME SO.

WHAT OF THAT, MY DEAR! HIS WEALTH IS OF NO USE TO HIM. HE DON'T DO ANY GOOD WITH IT.

HE DON'T MAKE HIMSELF COMFORTABLE WITH IT.

HE HASN'T THE SATISFACTION OF THINKING --

HA, HA, HA!

-- THAT HE IS EVER GOING TO BENEFIT US WITH IT.

I HAVE **NO PATIENCE** WITH HIM.

NEITHER DO I.

NOR ME.

OH, **I HAVE!** I AM **SORRY** FOR HIM; I COULDN'T BE **ANGRY** WITH HIM IF I **TRIED.**

WHO **SUFFERS** BY HIS **ILL WHIMS!** HIMSELF, ALWAYS. **HERE,** HE **TAKES IT** INTO HIS **HEAD** TO DISLIKE US, AND HE **WON'T** COME AND **DINE** WITH US.

WHAT'S THE **CONSEQUENCE?** HE DON'T **LOSE** MUCH OF A DINNER.

INDEED, I THINK HE **LOSES** A **VERY GOOD** DINNER.

WELL! I'M **VERY GLAD** TO **HEAR** IT, BECAUSE I HAVEN'T **GREAT FAITH** IN THESE **YOUNG HOUSEKEEPERS.**

WHAT DO **YOU** SAY, **TOPPER?**

DO GO ON, FRED. HE NEVER **FINISHES** WHAT HE BEGINS TO **SAY!** HE IS **SUCH A RIDICULOUS FELLOW!**

I WAS **GOING** TO SAY, THAT THE **CONSEQUENCE** OF HIS TAKING A **DISLIKE** TO US, AND **NOT** MAKING **MERRY** WITH US, **IS**, AS I **THINK**, THAT HE **LOSES** SOME PLEASANT MOMENTS, WHICH COULD DO HIM NO **HARM**.

I AM **SURE** HE LOSES PLEASANTER COMPANIONS THAN HE CAN FIND IN HIS **OWN** THOUGHTS, WITHER IN HIS **MOULDY** OLD OFFICE, OR HIS **DUSTY** CHAMBERS.

I MEAN TO GIVE HIM THE **SAME** CHANCE EVERY YEAR, WHETHER HE **LIKES** IT OR **NOT**, FOR I **PITY** HIM.

HE MAY **RAIL** AT CHRISTMAS TILL HE **DIES**, BUT HE **CAN'T** HELP THINKING **BETTER** OF IT -- I DEFY HIM -- IF HE FINDS ME **GOING** THERE, IN **GOOD** TEMPER, YEAR AFTER **YEAR**, AND SAYING **UNCLE SCROOGE,** HOW **ARE** YOU?

IF IT ONLY **PUTS** HIM IN THE **VEIN** TO LEAVE HIS POOR CLERK FIFTY POUNDS, THAT'S SOMETHING; AND I **THINK** I SHOOK HIM YESTERDAY.

HA, HA, HA!

HA, HA!

HA, HA!

IT WAS **THEIR** TURN TO **LAUGH** NOW, AT THE **NOTION** OF HIS **SHAKING** SCROOGE.

AFTER **TEA**, THEY HAD SOME **MUSIC**. SCROOGE SOFTENED **MORE** AND **MORE**.

BUT THEY **DIDN'T** DEVOTE THE **WHOLE EVENING** TO MUSIC.

AFTER A **WHILE**, THEY PLAYED AT **FORFEITS**, BUT **FIRST** THERE WAS A GAME OF **BLIND-MAN'S BUFF.**

I **NO MORE BELIEVE** THAT **TOPPER** WAS **REALLY BLIND** THAN I BELIEVE HE HAD **EYES** IN HIS **BOOTS.** THE **WAY** HE WENT AFTER THE **SAME** SISTER WAS AN **OUTRAGE** ON THE **CREDULITY** OF HUMAN NATURE.

PLEASE LET US **STAY** UNTIL THE **GUESTS** DEPART.

THAT **CANNOT** BE DONE.

HERE IS A NEW GAME. ONE HALF HOUR, SPIRIT, ONLY ONE!

91

MUCH THEY SAW, AND FAR THEY WENT, AND MANY HOMES THEY VISITED...

...BUT ALWAYS WITH A HAPPY END.

IT WAS A *LONG NIGHT*, IF IT WERE *ONLY* A NIGHT; BUT *SCROOGE* HAD HIS *DOUBTS* OF THIS, BECAUSE THE *CHRISTMAS HOLIDAYS* APPEARED TO BE CONDENSED INTO THE *SPACE* OF TIME THEY PASSED *TOGETHER*. WHILE SCROOGE REMAINED *UNALTERED* IN HIS OUTWARD FORM, THE *GHOST* GREW *CLEARLY OLDER*.

ARE *SPIRITS' LIVES* SO SHORT?

MY *LIFE UPON THIS GLOBE*, IS VERY BRIEF. IT ENDS *TO-NIGHT*.

TO-NIGHT!

TO-NIGHT AT MIDNIGHT.

HARK! THE TIME IS DRAWING NEAR.

FORGIVE ME IF I AM NOT *JUSTIFIED* IN WHAT I *ASK*, BUT I SEE SOMETHING *STRANGE*, AND NOT BELONGING TO *YOURSELF*, PROTRUDING FROM YOUR *SKIRTS*.

IS IT A FOOT OR A CLAW?

IT MIGHT BE A CLAW, FOR THE FLESH THERE IS *UPON* IT.

LOOK HERE.

DONG!
DONG!
DONG!
DONG!
DONG!
DONG!
DONG!
DONG!
DONG!
DONG!

THE **BELL** STRUCK **TWELVE.**

SCROOGE **LOOKED** FOR THE **GHOST,** AND **SAW** IT **NOT.**

AS THE LAST **STROKE** CEASED TO **VIBRATE,** HE **REMEMBERED** THE **PREDICTION** OF OLD **JACOB** MARLEY, AND **LIFTING UP** HIS **EYES, BEHELD...**

Stave Four: The Last of the Spirits

I AM IN THE **PRESENCE** OF THE **GHOST** OF **CHRISTMAS YET** TO **COME?**

THE **SPIRIT** DID NOT **ANSWER.**

95

THE GARMENT **CONTRACTED**, AS IF THE **SPIRIT** HAD **INCLINED** ITS **HEAD**.

THAT WAS THE **ONLY** ANSWER HE RECEIVED.

YOU ARE **ABOUT** TO **SHOW** ME **SHADOWS** OF THE **THINGS** THAT HAVE **NOT** HAPPENED --

-- BUT **WILL** HAPPEN IN THE **TIME** BEFORE US.

IS THAT **SO**, SPIRIT?

GHOST OF THE **FUTURE**! I **FEAR YOU** MORE THAN **ANY** SPECTRE I HAVE **SEEN**.

BUT AS I **KNOW** YOUR **PURPOSE** IS TO **DO ME GOOD**, AND AS I **HOPE** TO **LIVE** TO BE **ANOTHER MAN** FROM WHAT I **WAS**,

I AM **PREPARED** TO **BEAR YOU COMPANY**; AND **DO IT** WITH A **THANKFUL HEART**.

WILL YOU NOT **SPEAK** TO ME?

IT **GAVE** HIM **NO REPLY**.

SCROOGE *LOOKED ABOUT* FOR HIS *OWN IMAGE,* BUT SAW *NO LIKENESS* OF HIMSELF AMONG THE *MULTITUDES.*

THEY *LEFT* THE *BUSY SCENE,* AND WENT INTO AN *OBSCURE PART* OF THE *TOWN,* WHERE *SCROOGE* HAD *NEVER PENETRATED* BEFORE ALTHOUGH HE *RECOGNISED* ITS *SITUATION,* AND ITS *BAD REPUTE.*

ALLEYS AND *ARCHWAYS,* LIKE SO MANY *CESSPOOLS,* DISGORGED THEIR *OFFENCES* OF *SMELL,* AND *DIRT,* AND *LIFE,* UPON THE *STRAGGLING STREETS;*

AND THE WHOLE QUARTER *REEKED* WITH *CRIME,* WITH *FILTH,* AND *MISERY.*

FAR IN THIS *DEN* OF *INFAMOUS RESORT,* THERE WAS A LOW-BROWED, *BEETLING SHOP,* WHERE *IRON, OLD RAGS, BOTTLES, BONES* AND *GREASY OFFAL* WERE BOUGHT.

SITTING IN AMONG THE **WARES** HE **DEALT** IN, WAS A GREY-HAIRED **RASCAL**, WHO SMOKED HIS **PIPE** IN ALL THE **LUXURY** OF **CALM RETIREMENT.**

LOOK HERE, OLD **JOE**, HERE'S A **CHANCE!** IF WE HAVEN'T **ALL THREE MET HERE** WITHOUT **MEANING** IT!

YOU COULDN'T HAVE **MET** IN A **BETTER PLACE.** COME INTO THE **PARLOUR.**

STOP TILL I **SHUT** THE **DOOR** OF THE **SHOP.**

AH! HOW IT **SKREEKS!**

SCREEEECH!!

THERE **AIN'T** SUCH A **RUSTY BIT** OF **METAL** IN THE PLACE AS ITS **OWN** HINGES, I BELIEVE; AND I'M **SURE** THERE'S **NO SUCH OLD BONES** HERE, AS **MINE.**

HA, HA! WE'RE **ALL SUITABLE** TO OUR **CALLING,** WE'RE **WELL MATCHED.**

101

IF HE WANTED TO **KEEP** 'EM AFTER HE WAS **DEAD**, A WICKED OLD **SCREW**, WHY WASN'T HE **NATURAL** IN HIS **LIFETIME?**

IF HE **HAD** BEEN, HE'D HAVE **HAD SOMEBODY** TO LOOK AFTER HIM WHEN HE WAS **STRUCK** WITH **DEATH**, INSTEAD OF **LYING** GASPING OUT HIS **LAST** THERE, **ALONE** BY HIMSELF.

IT'S THE **TRUEST WORD** THAT EVER WAS **SPOKE**. IT'S A **JUDGMENT** ON HIM.

I WISH IT WAS A **LITTLE** HEAVIER ONE, AND IT **SHOULD** HAVE BEEN, YOU MAY **DEPEND** UPON IT,

IF I COULD HAVE **LAID MY HANDS** ON **ANYTHING ELSE** --

-- **OPEN** THAT **BUNDLE**, OLD JOE, AND LET ME **KNOW** THE **VALUE** OF IT. **SPEAK OUT** PLAIN.

I'M NOT **AFRAID** TO BE THE **FIRST**, NOR AFRAID FOR **THEM** TO **SEE** IT. WE KNEW PRETTY WELL THAT WE WERE **HELPING OURSELVES**, BEFORE WE MET HERE, I BELIEVE.

IT'S NO **SIN**. OPEN THE **BUNDLE**, JOE.

NO, LADY, LET **ME** BE THE **FIRST.**

THE **MAN** PRODUCED HIS **PLUNDER.**

IT WAS **NOT EXTENSIVE.**

103

PUTTING IT ON HIM TO BE BURIED IN, TO BE SURE. SOMEBODY WAS FOOL ENOUGH TO DO IT, BUT I TOOK IT OFF AGAIN.

IF CALICO AIN'T GOOD ENOUGH FOR SUCH A PURPOSE, IT ISN'T GOOD ENOUGH FOR ANYTHING.

IT'S QUITE AS BECOMING TO THE BODY. HE CAN'T LOOK UGLIER THAN HE DID IN THAT ONE.

HE, HA! THIS IS THE END OF IT, YOU SEE!

HE FRIGHTENED EVERY ONE AWAY FROM HIM WHEN HE WAS ALIVE, TO PROFIT US WHEN HE WAS DEAD! HA, HA, HA!

SPIRIT! I SEE; I SEE.

THE CASE OF THIS UNHAPPY MAN MIGHT BE MY OWN. MY LIFE TENDS THAT WAY; NOW.

MERCIFUL HEAVEN, WHAT IS THIS!

HE RECOILED IN TERROR, FOR THE SCENE HAD CHANGED...

107

...AND, WITHDRAWING IT, REVEALED A MOTHER AND HER CHILDREN.

KNOCK!
KNOCK!
KNOCK!

SHE WAS EXPECTING SOMEONE, WITH ANXIOUS EAGERNESS...

...IT WAS HER HUSBAND.

I DON'T **KNOW**. BUT **BEFORE** THAT TIME WE SHALL BE **READY** WITH THE **MONEY**; AND EVEN THOUGH WE WERE **NOT**, IT WOULD BE A **BAD** FORTUNE INDEED TO FIND SO MERCILESS A **CREDITOR** IN HIS **SUCCESSOR**.

WE MAY **SLEEP TO-NIGHT** WITH **LIGHT HEARTS**, CAROLINE!

THE **ONLY** EMOTION THAT THE **GHOST** COULD **SHOW** HIM, CAUSED BY THE **EVENT**, WAS ONE OF **PLEASURE**.

LET ME SEE SOME **TENDERNESS** CONNECTED WITH A **DEATH**, OR THAT **DARK CHAMBER**, SPIRIT, WHICH WE **LEFT** JUST NOW, WILL BE **FOR EVER PRESENT** TO ME.

THE GHOST **CONDUCTED HIM** THROUGH SEVERAL **STREETS** FAMILIAR TO HIS **FEET**; AND AS THEY WENT **ALONG**, SCROOGE LOOKED **HERE** AND **THERE** TO FIND HIMSELF, BUT **NOWHERE** WAS HE TO BE **SEEN**.

THEY ENTERED *BOB CRATCHIT'S* HOUSE; ALL WAS *QUIET.* VERY *QUIET.*

"And He took a child, and set him in the midst of them."

FROM WHERE DID I *HEAR* THOSE *WORDS?*

THE *COLOUR* HURTS MY *EYES.*

IT MAKES THEM *WEAK* BY *CANDLE-LIGHT;* AND I WOULDN'T SHOW *WEAK* EYES TO YOUR *FATHER* WHEN HE COMES HOME, FOR THE *WORLD.* IT *MUST* BE NEAR HIS *TIME.*

PAST IT RATHER. BUT I *THINK* HE'S WALKED A LITTLE *SLOWER* THAN HE USED; THESE *FEW* LAST EVENINGS, MOTHER.

I HAVE KNOWN HIM **WALK** WITH --

-- I HAVE **KNOWN** HIM **WALK** WITH *TINY TIM* UPON HIS SHOULDER, VERY FAST INDEED.

AND **SO HAVE I** - OFTEN.

BUT HE WAS **VERY LIGHT** TO **CARRY**, AND HIS **FATHER LOVED** HIM SO, THAT IT WAS **NO TROUBLE** --

-- **NO TROUBLE.**

AND **THERE IS** YOUR **FATHER** AT THE **DOOR!**

DON'T **MIND IT,** FATHER.

DON'T BE **GRIEVED!**

I MET SCROOGE'S NEPHEW TODAY, AND HE NOTICED THAT I LOOKED A LITTLE --

YOU LOOK JUST A LITTLE DOWN, YOU KNOW. WHAT HAS HAPPENED TO DISTRESS YOU?

ON WHICH, FOR HE IS THE PLEASANTEST-SPOKEN GENTLEMAN YOU EVER HEARD, I TOLD HIM WHAT HAD HAPPENED.

"I AM HEARTILY SORRY FOR IT, MR. CRATCHIT" HE SAID;

"AND HEARTILY SORRY FOR YOUR GOOD WIFE."

BY THE BYE, HOW HE EVER KNEW THAT, I DON'T KNOW.

KNEW WHAT, MY DEAR?

WHY, THAT YOU WERE A GOOD WIFE.

EVERYBODY KNOWS THAT!

VERY WELL OBSERVED, MY BOY!

I HOPE THEY DO.

"HEARTILY **SORRY**, FOR YOUR **GOOD** WIFE. IF I CAN BE OF **SERVICE** TO YOU IN **ANY WAY**", HE **SAID**, GIVING ME HIS **CARD**, "THAT'S WHERE I **LIVE**. PRAY **COME** TO ME."

NOW, IT **WASN'T**, FOR THE **SAKE** OF ANYTHING HE MIGHT BE ABLE TO **DO** FOR US, SO MUCH AS FOR HIS **KIND WAY**, THAT **THIS** WAS **QUITE DELIGHTFUL**.

IT **REALLY SEEMED** AS IF HE HAD **KNOWN** OUR **TINY TIM**, AND **FELT** WITH US.

I'M **SURE** HE'S A **GOOD SOUL**!

YOU WOULD BE **SURER** OF IT, MY **DEAR**, IF YOU **SAW** AND **SPOKE** TO HIM.

I SHOULDN'T BE AT **ALL** SURPRISED, **MARK** WHAT I **SAY**, IF HE GOT **PETER** A **BETTER SITUATION**.

ONLY **HEAR THAT**, PETER.

AND **THEN** PETER WILL BE **KEEPING COMPANY** WITH SOME ONE, AND **SETTING UP** FOR **HIMSELF**.

GET ALONG WITH YOU!

119

121

THE PHANTOM POINTED AS BEFORE.

BEFORE I DRAW NEARER TO THAT STONE TO WHICH YOU POINT, ANSWER ME ONE QUESTION.

ARE THESE THE SHADOWS OF THE THINGS THAT WILL BE, OR ARE THEY SHADOWS OF THINGS THAT MAY BE, ONLY?

YES! AND THE *BEDPOST* WAS HIS *OWN*. THE *BED* WAS HIS *OWN*, THE *ROOM* WAS HIS *OWN*.

BEST AND HAPPIEST OF *ALL*, THE *TIME BEFORE* HIM WAS HIS *OWN*, TO MAKE *AMENDS IN!*

I WILL *LIVE* IN THE *PAST*, THE *PRESENT*, AND THE *FUTURE!* THE *SPIRITS* OF *ALL THREE* SHALL *STRIVE WITHIN ME.*

OH, *JACOB MARLEY!* HEAVEN, AND THE *CHRISTMAS TIME* BE *PRAISED* FOR THIS!

I *SAY IT* ON MY *KNEES*, OLD *JACOB; ON MY KNEES!*

THEY ARE *NOT TORN DOWN*, THEY ARE *NOT* TORN DOWN, *RINGS* AND *ALL*.

THEY ARE *HERE* - *I* AM HERE - THE *SHADOWS* OF THE *THINGS* THAT *WOULD HAVE BEEN*, MAY BE *DISPELLED.*

129

131

I'LL **SEND IT** TO **BOB CRATCHIT'S!** HE SHAN'T KNOW WHO **SENDS** IT. IT'S **TWICE** THE **SIZE** OF **TINY TIM.**

JOE MILLER NEVER MADE SUCH A **JOKE** AS SENDING IT TO **BOB'S** WILL BE!

HE WROTE THE **ADDRESS,** AND WENT **DOWN STAIRS** TO OPEN THE **STREET DOOR,** READY FOR THE **ARRIVAL OF** THE **POULTERER'S MAN.**

AS HE **STOOD** THERE, THE **KNOCKER** CAUGHT HIS **EYE.**

I SHALL **LOVE IT,** AS LONG AS I **LIVE!**

I **SCARCELY** EVER **LOOKED** AT IT **BEFORE.** WHAT AN **HONEST** EXPRESSION IT HAS IN ITS **FACE!** IT'S A **WONDERFUL KNOCKER!**

HERE'S THE **TURKEY.**

HALLO! WHOOP! HOW **ARE YOU!** MERRY CHRISTMAS!

WHY, IT'S **IMPOSSIBLE** TO **CARRY** THAT TO **CAMDEN TOWN.**

YOU MUST HAVE A **CAB.**

HE, HE, HE!

THE **CHUCKLE** WITH WHICH HE DID ALL THIS WAS **ONLY EXCEEDED**...

...BY THE **CHUCKLE** WITH WHICH HE SAT DOWN **BREATHLESS** IN HIS **CHAIR** AGAIN, AND **CHUCKLED** TILL HE **CRIED**.

HE **DRESSED** HIMSELF "**ALL IN HIS BEST**"...

...AND AT LAST GOT **OUT** INTO THE **STREETS**.

GOOD **MORNING, SIR!** A **MERRY CHRISTMAS** TO YOU!

A **MERRY CHRISTMAS** TO YOU TOO, SIR!

MY **DEAR** SIR. HOW **DO** YOU **DO**? I HOPE YOU **SUCCEEDED** YESTERDAY. IT WAS VERY **KIND** OF YOU.

A **MERRY CHRISTMAS** TO YOU, SIR!

MR. **SCROOGE**?

YES. THAT IS MY **NAME**, AND I FEAR IT MAY **NOT** BE PLEASANT TO YOU. ALLOW ME TO **ASK** YOUR **PARDON.**

And will you have the goodness...

LORD **BLESS** ME! MY **DEAR** MR. **SCROOGE**, ARE YOU **SERIOUS**?

IF YOU **PLEASE.** NOT A **FARTHING LESS.**

A **GREAT MANY BACK-PAYMENTS** ARE INCLUDED IN IT, I ASSURE YOU.

WILL YOU DO ME THAT **FAVOUR**?

MY **DEAR** SIR, I DON'T KNOW **WHAT** TO SAY TO SUCH **MUNIFI**...

DON'T **SAY** ANYTHING, PLEASE. **COME** AND **SEE** ME.

WILL YOU **COME** AND **SEE** ME?

I **WILL**!

THANK'EE, I AM **MUCH OBLIGED** TO YOU. I THANK YOU **FIFTY TIMES**.

BLESS YOU!

HE WENT TO *CHURCH*, AND *WALKED* ABOUT THE *STREETS*, AND *WATCHED* THE PEOPLE HURRYING *TO* AND *FRO*...

...AND QUESTIONED *BEGGARS*, AND LOOKED *DOWN* INTO THE *KITCHENS* OF *HOUSES*...

...AND PATTED *CHILDREN* ON THE *HEAD*...

...AND FOUND THAT *EVERYTHING* COULD YIELD HIM *PLEASURE*.

IN THE *AFTERNOON*, HE TURNED HIS *STEPS* TOWARDS HIS *NEPHEW'S* HOUSE.

IS YOUR *MASTER* AT *HOME*, MY *DEAR*?

YES, SIR.

WHERE *IS HE*, MY *LOVE*?

HE'S IN THE *DINING-ROOM*, SIR, ALONG WITH *MISTRESS*.

I'LL *SHOW* YOU *UP-STAIRS*, IF YOU PLEASE.

THANK'EE. HE *KNOWS* ME. I'LL GO IN *HERE*, MY *DEAR*.

135

I'LL **RAISE** YOUR **SALARY;** AND ENDEAVOUR TO ASSIST YOUR **STRUGGLING FAMILY,** AND WE WILL **DISCUSS** YOUR **AFFAIRS** THIS **VERY AFTERNOON,** OVER A CHRISTMAS BOWL OF SMOKING BISHOP, BOB!

MAKE **UP** THE **FIRES,** AND BUY **ANOTHER COAL-SCUTTLE** BEFORE YOU **DOT** ANOTHER **I,** BOB CRATCHIT!

SCROOGE WAS **BETTER** THAN HIS **WORD.**

HE DID IT **ALL,** AND **INFINITELY MORE;** AND TO **TINY TIM,** WHO **DID NOT DIE,** HE WAS A **SECOND FATHER.**

HE **BECAME** AS GOOD A **FRIEND,** AS GOOD A **MASTER,** AND AS GOOD A **MAN** AS THE GOOD OLD CITY **KNEW,** OR **ANY OTHER** GOOD OLD CITY, TOWN, OR **BOROUGH,** IN THE GOOD OLD **WORLD.**

SOME PEOPLE **LAUGHED** TO SEE THE **ALTERATION** IN HIM, BUT HE **LET** THEM **LAUGH,** AND **LITTLE HEEDED** THEM; FOR HE WAS **WISE ENOUGH** TO **KNOW** THAT **NOTHING** EVER **HAPPENED** ON THIS **GLOBE,** FOR **GOOD,** AT WHICH **SOME** PEOPLE DID NOT **HAVE** THEIR **FILL** OF **LAUGHTER** IN THE **OUTSET;**

AND **KNOWING** THAT SUCH AS **THESE** WOULD BE **BLIND ANYWAY,** HE THOUGHT IT **QUITE** AS **WELL** THAT THEY SHOULD **WRINKLE** UP THEIR **EYES** IN **GRINS,** AS HAVE THE **MALADY** IN **LESS ATTRACTIVE** FORMS.

HIS **OWN HEART** LAUGHED; AND **THAT** WAS **QUITE ENOUGH** FOR HIM.

HE HAD **NO FURTHER** INTERCOURSE WITH **SPIRITS,** BUT **LIVED** UPON THE **TOTAL ABSTINENCE** PRINCIPLE, EVER **AFTERWARDS;** AND IT WAS **ALWAYS SAID** OF HIM, THAT HE **KNEW** HOW TO **KEEP CHRISTMAS WELL,** IF **ANY** MAN **ALIVE** POSSESSED THE KNOWLEDGE.

MAY **THAT** BE **TRULY SAID** OF US, AND **ALL** OF US! AND **SO,** AS TINY TIM OBSERVED...

GOD BLESS US, EVERY ONE!

A Christmas Carol

The End

"It was the best of times, it was the worst of times, it was the age of wisdom, it was the age of foolishness, it was the epoch of belief, it was the epoch of incredulity, it was the season of Light, it was the season of Darkness, it was the spring of hope, it was the winter of despair, we had everything before us, we had nothing before us, we were all going direct to Heaven, we were all going direct the other way – in short, the period was so far like the present period, that some of its noisiest authorities insisted on its being received, for good or for evil, in the superlative degree of comparison only."

Excerpt from *A Tale of Two Cities* by Charles Dickens

143

What the Dickens?

(1812 - 1870 AD)

Charles John Huffam Dickens was born in Landport, Portsmouth, on 7th February 1812. He was the second of eight children born to John and Elizabeth Dickens, and described himself as a "very small and not-over-particularly-taken-care-of boy". Although not wealthy, the Dickens family was not poor. They moved to Chatham, Kent in 1817 and sent Charles to the fee paying William Giles' school in the area. Despite his youth, he was a frequent visitor to the theatre. He enjoyed Shakespeare, and claimed to have learned many things from watching plays.

By the time he was ten, the family had moved again; this time to London following the career of his father, John, who was a clerk in the Naval Pay Office. John had a poor head for money, but liked to impress people. As a result, he got into debt and was sent to Marshalsea Prison in 1824. His wife and most of the children joined him there (a common occurrence in those days before the Bankruptcy Act of 1869 abolished debtors' prisons). Charles, however, was put to work at Warren's Blacking Factory, where he labelled jars of boot polish.

Later in 1824, John's mother died and left enough money to her son to pay off his debts and get

Charles Dickens

him released. John Dickens retired from the Navy Pay Office later that year and worked as a reporter for *The Mirror of Parliament*, where his brother-in-law was editor. He allowed Charles to leave Warren's Blacking Factory, and go back to school. Charles' brief time at the factory continued to haunt him for the rest of his life. He later wrote:

"For many years, when I came near to Robert Warren's, in the Strand, I crossed over to the opposite side of the way, to avoid a certain smell of the cement they put upon the blacking corks, which reminded me of what I

once was. My old way home by the borough made me cry, after my oldest child could speak."

Dickens Fact

"Dicken" or "Dickens" was used as another name for the Devil. The first recorded use appears to have been by William Shakespeare in *The Merry Wives of Windsor*.

FORD:
 Where had you this pretty weathercock?

MRS PAGE:
 I cannot tell what the dickens his name is my husband had him of.

Charles left school at fifteen and worked as an office boy with a Mr. Molloy of Lincoln's Inn. Here, he decided to be a journalist. He studied shorthand at night, and went on to spend two years as a shorthand reporter at the Doctors' Commons Courts. Many thought that the institution of Doctors' Commons (a society of lawyers in London) was old-fashioned and ridiculous - including Dickens: his satirical description of his time there can be found in both *Sketches by Boz* and in *David Copperfield*.

Charles' first love was Maria Beadnell — a banker's daughter whom he met in 1830. Their relationship came to an end after three years, probably through the wishes of Maria's parents who thought that Charles was not good enough for their daughter.

Around this time, Dickens started to achieve recognition for his own written work. He wrote for a number of newspapers: *True Sun* (1830-32), *Mirror of Parliament* (1832-34), and *The Morning Chronicle* (1834-36). He was later to recognise how important these

years were to him, when he wrote, "To the wholesome training of severe newspaper work, when I was a very young man, I constantly refer my first successes".

December 1833 saw his first published (but unpaid for) work appear in *The Old Monthly* magazine: a story entitled *A Dinner at Poplar Walk*. On seeing his first work in print, Dickens wrote, "On which occasion I walked down to Westminster-hall, and turned into it for half an hour, because my eyes were so dimmed with joy and pride, that they could not bear the street, and were not fit to be seen there".

He wrote further stories for *The Old Monthly*, but when the magazine could not pay for them, Dickens began to write his "series" for *The Chronicle* at the request of

their editor, George Hogarth. In 1835, Charles got engaged to George Hogarth's eldest daughter, Catherine. They married on 2nd April 1836 and went on to have ten children (seven boys and three girls). Biographers have long suspected that Dickens preferred Catherine's sister, Mary, who lived with the Dickens family and died in his arms in 1837 at the age of seventeen. Dickens had asked to be buried next to her; but when her brother died in 1841, Dickens' "place" was taken. He wrote to his great friend and biographer John Forster,

"It is a great trial for me to give up Mary's grave... the desire to be buried next to her is as strong upon me now, as it was five years ago... And I know...that it will never diminish...I cannot bear the thought of being excluded from her dust".

Not only did Dickens wear her ring for the rest of his life, he also wrote the epitaph which appears on her gravestone:

"Young, beautiful, and good, God numbered her among his angels at the early age of seventeen".

In 1844, another of Catherine's sisters, Georgina, moved in to the Dickens household; some say that the novelist fell in love with her too.

145

The first series of *Sketches by Boz* was published in 1836. "Boz" was an early pen name used by Dickens. It came from

> "the nickname of a pet child, a younger brother, whom I had dubbed Moses, in honour of The Vicar of Wakefield, which, being pronounced Bozes, got shortened into Boz".

Shortly afterwards, with the success of *Pickwick Papers* in 1837, Dickens was at last a full-time novelist. He produced works at an incredible rate; and at the start of

his writing career, also continued his work as a journalist and editor. He began his next book, *Oliver Twist*, in 1837 and continued it in monthly parts until April 1839.

Dickens visited Canada and the United States in 1842, taking Catherine and her maid with him. During that visit he talked on the need for international copyright, because some American publishers were printing his books without his permission and without any payment; he also

talked about the need to end slavery. His visit and his opinions were recorded and published as *American Notes* in October of that year, causing quite a stir.

17th December 1843 saw the publication of *A Christmas Carol*. It was the first of Dickens' enormously successful series of Christmas books which ran until 1848. It was so popular that it sold five-thousand copies by Christmas Eve – and has never been out of print since.

Dickens became something of an international celebrity. In 1853 he toured Italy with his friends Augustus Egg (the artist), and Wilkie Collins (the author and playwright). On his return to England, he gave the first of many public readings from his own works: at first he did these for charity, but before long he demanded payment.

From childhood, Dickens had loved the stage and enjoyed the attention and applause he received. He performed in amateur theatre throughout the 1840s and 50s, and formed his own amateur theatrical company in 1845, which occupied much of his time.

By 1856, Dickens had made enough money to purchase a fine country house: Gads Hill in Kent. He had admired this place ever since his arrival to the area as a child, and it must have felt a huge achievement to finally own it. However, Gads Hill was not a happy family home. A year later, Charles met a young actress called Ellen Lawless Ternan who went on to join his theatre company; and they began a relationship that was to last until his death.

Charles separated from his wife Catherine in 1858. The event was talked about in the newspapers, and Dickens publicly denied rumours of an affair. He was morally trapped — he was deeply in love with Ellen, but his writing career was based on promoting family values and being a good person; he felt that if he admitted his relationship with Ellen, it would put an end to his writing career.

Catherine moved to a house in London with their eldest son Charles, and Dickens remained at Gads Hill with the rest of the children and Catherine's sister, Georgina (there were rumours of Charles and Georgina having a relationship too). On her deathbed in 1879 Catherine gave her collection of Dickens' letters to her daughter Kate, instructing her to:

> "Give these to the British Museum, that the world may know he loved me once".

The more he tried to hide his personal life, the more it came out in his writing. One of his most popular books, *Great Expectations* (1860) has elements of imprisonment, love that can never be, people living in isolation, and the urge to better oneself — all subjects that were part of Dickens' own life at the time.

He looked after Ellen until his death, renting houses for her to live in, and making regular secret journeys to see her — not easy for the local celebrity that Dickens had become. He went to incredible lengths to keep his secret safe, including renting houses under different names and setting up offices for his business in places that made it easy for him to visit her. On 4th September 1860 he wrote to William Henry Wills, the sub-editor of *Household Words*:

> "Yesterday I burnt, in the field at Gads Hill, the accumulated letters and papers of twenty years. They set up a smoke like the genie when he got out of the casket on the seashore; and as it was an exquisite day when I began, and rained very heavily when I

finished, I suspect my correspondence of having overcast the face of the heavens".

In 1865, Dickens was involved in the Staplehurst Rail Crash: an incident which disturbed him greatly. He was travelling by train, along with Ellen and her mother: they were most likely returning from a secret holiday in France. The train left the track, resulting in the deaths of ten people, with a further forty being injured. It is reported that Dickens tended to some of the wounded. He wrote to his old friend Thomas Mitton about the crash:

> "My dear Mitton,
> I should have written to you yesterday or the day before, if I had been quite up to writing. I am a little shaken, not by the beating and dragging of the carriage in which I was, but by the hard work afterwards in getting out the dying and dead, which was most horrible.
> Two ladies were my fellow passengers; an old one, and a young one.
> I don't want to be examined at the Inquests and I don't want to write about it. It could do no good either way, and I could only

seem to speak about myself, which, of course, I would rather not do".

Even when writing to a friend, Dickens still hid Ellen's name, and he didn't want to be part of the inquest in case his relationship became public knowledge.

By 1867 Dickens' health was getting worse. His doctor advised him to rest, but he carried on with his busy schedule, including another tour of America.

Mark Twain saw him during this second American tour in January 1868 and wrote:

"Promptly at 8pm, unannounced, and without waiting for any stamping or clapping of hands to call him out, a tall, "spry," (if I may say it,) thin-legged old gentleman, gotten up regardless of expense, especially as to shirt-front and diamonds, with a bright red flower in his button-hole, gray beard and moustache, bald head, and with side hair brushed fiercely and tempestuously forward, as if its owner were sweeping down before a gale of wind, the very Dickens came! He did not emerge upon the stage – that is rather too deliberate a word – he strode."

By the end of this tour, it is said that Dickens was so ill that he could hardly eat solid food, surviving on champagne and eggs beaten in sherry. He returned to England and despite his bad health, continued his public reading appearances. In April 1869, he collapsed during a reading at Preston, and he was again advised to rest. Dickens didn't listen, and continued to give performances in London as well as starting work on a new novel, *The Mystery of Edwin Drood*.

This novel was never finished: Dickens had a stroke and died suddenly at Gads Hill on 9th June 1870. He had asked to be buried "in an inexpensive, unostentatious, and strictly private manner", but public opinion, led by *The Times* newspaper, insisted that he should be buried in keeping with his status as a great writer. He was buried at Westminster Abbey on 14th June 1870.

His funeral was a private affair, attended by just twelve mourners. After the service his grave was left open, and thousands of people from all walks of life came to pay their respects and throw flowers onto the coffin. Today, a small stone with a simple inscription marks his grave:

"CHARLES DICKENS BORN 7th FEBRUARY 1812 DIED 9th JUNE 1870"

Dickens was so closely associated with Christmas that, shortly after his death, the critic and poet Theodore Watts-Dunton overheard a London barrow girl say, **"Dickens dead? Then will Father Christmas die too?"**.

The Dickens Family Tree

Key:
Parent of ———
Married ═══

William Dickens
d. 1785

Elizabeth Ball
d. 1824

Charles Barrow
1759–1826
m. 1788

Mary Culliford
1771–1851

Mary Barrow
?

Thomas Culliford Barrow
1793–1857

Other children

William Dickens
1783–1826

John Dickens
1785–1851
m. 1809

Elizabeth Barrow
1789–1863

Frances Elizabeth Dickens
1810–1848

Alfred Dickens
b. & d. 1814

Letitia Mary Dickens
1816–1874

Harriet Ellen Dickens
b. & d. 1819

Frederick William Dickens
1820–1868

Alfred Lamerte Dickens
1822–1860

Augustus Dickens
1827–1868

George Hogarth
1783–1870
m. 1814

Georgina Thomson
1793–1863

Charles John Huffam Dickens
1812–1870
m. 1836

Catherine Thomson Hogarth
1815–1879

Mary Hogarth
1819–1837

Georgina Hogarth
1827–1917

Other children

Charles Culliford Boz Dickens
1837–1896

Kate Macready Dickens
1839–1929

Francis Jeffrey Dickens
1844–1886

Sydney Smith Haldimand Dickens
1847–1872

Dora Annie Dickens
1850–1851

Mary Dickens
1838–1896

Walter Landor Dickens
1841–1863

Alfred Tennyson Dickens
1845–1912

Henry Fielding Dickens
1849–1933

Edward Bulwer Lytton Dickens
1852–1902

Due to the lack of official records of births, deaths and marriages within this period, the above information is derived from extensive research and is as accurate as possible from the limited sources available.

Dickens Timeline

1812

7th February: Charles John Huffam Dickens born at Landport, Portsmouth.

1817

April: Family moves to Chatham, Kent.

1821

March: Charles goes to school (William Giles' school, next-door to the family home).

1822

September: Family moves to Camden Town, London.

1824

February: Charles (aged 12), goes to work at Warren's Blacking Factory. Charles' father arrested for debt and sent with his family to Marshalsea Prison.

May: Father and family released from prison.

June: Charles leaves the Blacking Factory and is enrolled in Wellington House Academy.

1827

May: Becomes an office boy for solicitors in Lincoln's Inn, and studies shorthand.

1828

November: Becomes a freelance reporter at Doctors' Commons courts.

1830

Becomes a parliamentary reporter for the *True Sun* newspaper.

1832

March: Moves to the *Mirror of Parliament* newspaper.

1833

December: First published story *A Dinner at Poplar Walk* appears in *The Old Monthly Magazine*.

1834

August: Moves to the *Morning Chronicle* newspaper, and writes under the name of "Boz".

November: Father once again arrested for debt; Charles comes to his aid.

1836

February: His first series of *Sketches by Boz* published; receives £150 for the copyright.

March: First part of *Pickwick Papers* appears in its serialised form, and runs for a year.

April: Marries Catherine Hogarth, daughter of George Hogarth, editor of the *Evening Chronicle*.

December: Becomes editor of *Bentley's Miscellany*, and publishes the second series of *Sketches by Boz*.

1837

February: Begins *Oliver Twist*, which continues in monthly parts in *Bentley's Miscellany* until 1839.

May: Catherine's younger sister Mary, whom he idolises, dies.

1838

March: Begins serialisation of *Nicholas Nickleby*, which continues until 1839.

1839

January: Resigns as editor of *Bentley's Miscellany*.

1840

April: Begins serialisation of *The Old Curiosity Shop*, which runs for a year in *Master Humphrey's Clock*.

1842

January: Travels to Canada and United States.

June: Returns to London and declines offer to stand for Parliament

October: Begins *American Notes*.

1843

January: Serialisation of *Martin Chuzzlewit* begins.

December: Publishes *A Christmas Carol*, the first of his Christmas books.

1845

September: His amateur theatrical company gives its first performance *(Every Man in his Humour)*.

1846

July: Begins *Dombey and Son*, which runs until April 1848.

1848

December: Publishes final Christmas book, *The Haunted Man*.

1849

May: *David Copperfield* serialised in monthly parts until November 1850.

1851

March: His father dies.

April: Death of his infant daughter, Dora.

1852

March: First appearance of *Bleak House*.

1853

December: Gives first public reading, for charity, of *A Christmas Carol* in Birmingham.

The Dickens Dramatical Company in 1854 with Charles Dickens at the front.

1854

April-August: *Hard Times* appears weekly in *Household Words*.

1855

December: *Little Dorrit* appears in monthly parts until 1857.

1856

March: Purchases Gads Hill, in Rochester, Kent.

1857

July: Performs in front of Queen Victoria.

August: Meets and falls in love with a young actress, Ellen Ternan.

1858

April: Dickens starts series of public readings for profit in London, and continues with a provincial tour.

May: Separates from his wife, Catherine. Her sister Georgina looks after the household.

1860

September: Dickens intentionally burns a large number of his personal letters.

December: Begins writing *Great Expectations*.

1863

September: His mother, Elizabeth Dickens, dies.

December: His son Walter dies in India.

1864

February: His health begins to fail, probably due to over work.

May: *Our Mutual Friend* begins in monthly parts and runs until 1865.

1865

June: Badly shaken after being involved in the Staplehurst Railway Accident, while travelling back from France with Ellen Ternan and her mother.

1867

November: Against doctors' advice, Dickens continues public readings in England and Ireland, and embarks on an American reading tour.

1868

April: Returns to England, and continues his series of readings.

November: His readings now include a sensational version of the death of Nancy in *Oliver Twist*.

1869

Dickens shows symptoms of having suffered a mild stroke. He cancels his provincial readings.

September: Begins to write *The Mystery of Edwin Drood*, and draws up his will.

1870

March: Has a private audience with Queen Victoria. His final public readings take place in London.

9th June: Dies at Gads Hill after suffering a stroke. He is buried on 14th June at Westminster Abbey.

September: Last of his unfinished *The Mystery of Edwin Drood* appears.

Hard Times

The Victorian era, 1837-1901, represented the height of the Industrial Revolution - a period of major social, economic, and technological advancement in Great Britain. Queen Victoria's reign also saw a huge expansion of the British Empire, making Britain the most important global power of the age.

It was a time of inventors and inventions; of rapid progress in science, technology and medicine, such as anaesthetics and antiseptics. From the steam engine to the steam printer, the skyscraper to the machine-gun, the flush toilet, photography, moving pictures, electricity, the telegraph and telephone — it was as if the Victorian era was a transition from the old traditional world into the new modern age.

Travel was also revolutionised, mainly through the rise of the railway as a method of transporting goods and people. Although the first purpose-built railway, from Stockton to Darlington, opened in 1825 (twelve years before Victoria became queen) the early years of her reign witnessed the most extraordinary boom — so called, "Railway Fever". In 1850, there were ten thousand miles of railway track in Britain; by 1901, that number had grown to about thirty-five thousand. The railway age changed the way people lived and worked.

The Royal Collection © 2008 Her Majesty Queen Elizabeth II

Queen Victoria

Many important developments, such as the fledgling postal service (the "Penny Post"), could not have happened without railways; and as technology allowed us to travel further and faster, the world was divided into twenty-four time zones — with Greenwich becoming the centre of the world's time.

But this new Britain was not a paradise for all: with this rapid progress came massive change in terms of population size, trades and the way in which people lived. The population trebled in Great Britain between 1800 and 1900 and people flocked to the cities to work in the new industries. Accommodation became overcrowded and unsanitary, with London being the area most affected. Much prosperity was generated for the elite through new technology, and on an underpaid workforce consisting of adults and children living in poverty. Millions of workers lived in slums or in old decaying houses. They had no sanitation, no fresh water supply, no paved streets, no schools, no law or order, no decent food and little fuel for fires.

Children were expected to earn wages to help the family; as Dickens himself did in Warren's Blacking Factory. They often worked long hours in dangerous jobs and in appalling conditions for just a few pennies a day.

There were also many homeless children who could only survive by begging and stealing. To the respectable Victorians they must have seemed a real threat to society; and something had to be done about them to preserve law and order.

Many believed that education was the answer, and a number of "Ragged Schools" were started to help meet that need. These were charitable schools dedicated to the free education of destitute children, and they often provided food, clothing and lodging on top of basic education. Charles Dickens' visit to Field Lane Ragged School in 1843 made a lasting impact on him, and it is said to have been a major influence when he wrote *A Christmas Carol*.

In 1870 an act of parliament allowed "Board Schools" to be paid for out of local rates, which allowed more children to attend school. However, it took another eleven years before schooling up to the age of ten became compulsory (1881), and a further nine years after that until state education became free for everyone (1890).

The government also began to protect the welfare of children in the workplace. The first Factory Act (1819) prohibited children under the age of nine from working in factories and those aged from nine to sixteen from working more than seventy-two hours per week.

In 1833, a second act limited the working hours for nine- to thirteen-year-olds in textile factories to a maximum of forty-eight hours per week. The Mines Act of 1842 stopped women and boys under ten from working underground. Further Factory Acts in 1844 and 1847 established the twelve-hour day for women and the six-and-a-half-hour day for children under thirteen. These laws were enforced by factory inspectors; but they were so poorly paid that they were easily bribed. In addition, many parents were so desperate for money that they lied about the ages of their children so that they could work. Before 1837 births didn't have to be registered, and without a birth certificate, it was impossible for anyone to prove the age of a child.

Life was indeed harsh. As well as appalling working conditions, low wages, slum housing and disease, the majority of the population had no means by which to change their circumstances; and nowhere was this better described than in the writings of Charles Dickens.

Dickens Fact

"Dickensian" = denoting poverty, distress, and exploitation, as depicted in the novels of Charles Dickens.

A Very Victorian Christmas

Prior to the arrival of Christianity in northern Europe, a twelve-day mid-winter "Yule" festival was celebrated, beginning the traditions of using evergreen plants like mistletoe, holly and ivy for decorations, and the burning of the yule log. With the introduction of the Julian calendar, this festival was fixed on 25th December and was combined with Christian celebrations to create the twelve days of what we now call Christmas.

Re-inventing Christmas

The Victorian era saw the re-invention of Christmas in Britain. When Queen Victoria's reign began in 1837, the celebration of Christmas was in decline. Nobody in Britain had heard of Santa Claus; Christmas cards and crackers had not been thought of; and most people were not allowed the time off from work or had the money with which to buy gifts or extra food — but this all began to change.

The wealth generated by the new factories and industries now gave middle class families the opportunity to take time off work and celebrate the festive season over Christmas Day and Boxing Day. The advent of the railways also allowed the country folk, who had moved into the towns and cities in search of work, to return home for a family Christmas.

Children's toys that used to be handmade and expensive were suddenly made more affordable through mass-production in factories. However, they were still too expensive for working families and the poor, whose Christmas stockings, (which first became popular around 1870), would contain only an apple, orange and a few nuts, or maybe a small home-made gift.

Food was a major part of the festivities. In northern England roast beef was the traditional fare for Christmas dinner while in London and the south, goose was favoured. Many of the poor had to make do with rabbit. It wasn't until the end of the century that most people had turkey for their Christmas dinner.

The introduction of a national postal service in 1840 (the "Penny Post") paved the way for the sending of Christmas cards. The first Christmas card was created in 1843 by Sir Henry Cole, a wealthy British businessman, who wanted a card that he could send to friends and professional acquaintances to wish them a "Merry Christmas".

In 1846, Tom Smith, a London sweet maker, made the first Christmas cracker. The original idea was to wrap his sweets in a twist of fancy coloured paper, but he found that they were more popular when he added mottos, paper hats and small toys; and especially when he devised a way to make the parcel open with a bang!

A Royal Celebration

Queen Victoria loved celebrating Christmas, which she described as a "most dear happy time". With nine children, her Christmases became great family occasions and many of the royal Christmas traditions were described in her personal diaries and in the newspapers of the day. These traditions included decorated trees, the sending of cards, a lavish family meal, and taking gifts to the poor. It was Queen Charlotte (Queen Victoria's grandmother, and wife of George III) who brought the German tradition of Christmas trees to England, and they were a feature of Victoria's Christmas festivities from childhood.

In her journal for Christmas Eve 1832, the thirteen-year-old Princess Victoria wrote:

> "After dinner... we then went into the drawing-room near the dining-room... There were two large round tables on which were placed two trees hung with lights and sugar ornaments. All the presents being placed round the trees..."

And for those less fortunate?

The Victorian era was one of stark contrasts, and Christmas was no exception. For the very poor, the passing of the Christmas season made little difference to their lives.

Following the example set by Queen Victoria, it became fashionable amongst the Victorian middle-classes to give "alms" to the poor (which is what the businessmen are trying to organise with Scrooge on page seventeen). The custom of giving gifts and food to the poor on Boxing Day (26th December) was also revived in this period, when the churches opened their alms boxes and distributed money to the poor.

For those without employment or homes of their own, the workhouse provided the venue for Christmas celebrations. In the era of the parish workhouse, prior to 1834, Christmas Day meant a treat for most of the residents. However, with the advent of union workhouses set up by the 1834 Poor Law Amendment Act, no extra food

was to be allowed on Christmas Day (or any other feast day). Despite that, Christmas Day was one of the special days when the workhouse inmates rested. It took six years for the rules to be revised to allow extra treats – but only if they came from private sources and not from union funds. A change in the ruling seven years later, in 1847, finally allowed the provision of Christmas extras from the workhouse funds.

With the exception of the very poor, Victorian Christmases were a time of celebration, and of families gathering together with the prospect of a feast (however small) and entertainment - all of which is captured in the most famous "Christmas Book" of all time.

A Christmas Carol

Dickens' first "Christmas Book", the best loved and most read of all of his books, began life as seeds planted in Dickens' mind during his travels around England, where he saw children working in

appalling conditions. His belief that education was a remedy for crime and poverty, along with scenes he had recently witnessed at the Field Lane Ragged School, made Dickens resolve to **"strike a sledge hammer blow"** for the poor.

As the idea for the story took shape and the writing began in earnest, Dickens became engrossed in the book. He later wrote that as the tale unfolded, he:
"wept and laughed, and wept again"

and that
> **"thinking whereof he walked about the black streets of London fifteen or twenty miles many a night when all of the sober folks had gone to bed".**

A Christmas Carol took just six weeks to complete, and the book was published on 17th December 1843. It was an overwhelming success, selling over five-thousand copies by Christmas Eve.

It is a book of enduring appeal that, due in no small part to the era of its release, has for many people become part of the festival of Christmas itself, and is one of the best-loved Christmas stories in the world.

Page Creation

1. Script

In order to create two versions of the same book, the story is first adapted into two scripts: Original Text and Quick Text. While the degree of complexity changes for each script, the artwork remains the same for both books.

Panel 1: Wide shot of the room, with Scrooge and ghost small within it, to leave room for the big speech balloons.		
SCROOGE	You travel fast?	You travel fast?
MARLEY'S GHOST	On the wings of the wind.	Very!
SCROOGE	You might have got over a great quantity of ground in seven years.	Then you must have gone far in seven years.
MARLEY'S GHOST	Oh! Captive, bound, and double-ironed, not to know that ages of incessant labour, by immortal creatures, for this earth must pass into eternity before the good of which it is susceptible is all developed.	Oh! Chained and bound. I didn't know that life is so short.
MARLEY'S GHOST (2nd Bubble)	Not to know that any Christian spirit working kindly in its little sphere, whatever it may be, will find its mortal life too short for its vast means of usefulness. Not to know that no space of regret can make amends for one life's opportunity misused!	And no amount of regret can make up for a lifetime lost.
Panel 2:		
MARLEY'S GHOST	Yet such was I! Oh! Such was I!	Yet, that was my life.
SCROOGE	But you were always a good man of business, Jacob.	You were good at business, Jacob.
Panel 3: Hand in a downward stroke, a dismissive gesture, as if the very word was dirty!		
MARLEY'S GHOST	Business!	Business!
Panel 4: The Ghost, wringing its hands		
MARLEY'S GHOST	Mankind was my business.	Mankind was my business.
	The common welfare was my business; charity, mercy, forbearance, and benevolence, were, all, my business. The dealings of my trade were but a drop of water in the comprehensive ocean of my business!	My work was nothing compared to the good of mankind.
Panel 5: It holds up its chain at arm's length, and then flings it heavily upon the ground again.		
SFX	CLANK !!! (loud)	CLANK !!! (loud)

A page from the script of *A Christmas Carol* showing the two versions of text.

2. Rough Sketch

The artist first creates a rough sketch from the panel directions provided by the scriptwriter. The artist is considering many things at this stage, including story pacing, emphasis of certain elements to tell the story in the best way, and even lighting of the scene.

The rough sketch created from the above script.

3. Pencils

Once a clear direction is established, the artist creates a pencil drawing of the page.

It is interesting to see the changes made from the rough to the pencil, such as in the last panel, where Marley's Ghost's movement has been increased to heighten the drama.

The pencil drawing of page 36.

4. Inks

From the pencil sketch an inked version of the same page is created. Inking is not simply tracing over the pencil

sketch, it is the process of using black ink to fill in the shaded areas and to add clarity and cohesion to the "pencils". The "inks" give us the final linework prior to the colouring stage.

The inked image, ready to be coloured.

5. Colouring

Adding colour really brings the page and its characters to life.

There is far more to the colouring stage than simply replacing the white areas with colour. Some of the linework is replaced with colour, the light sources are considered for shadows and highlights, and effects added. Finally, the whole page is colour-balanced to the other pages of that scene, and to the overall book.

6. Lettering

The final stage is to add the captions, sound effects, and dialogue speech bubbles from the script. These are laid on top of the finished coloured pages. Two versions of each page are lettered, one for each of the two versions of the book (Original Text and Quick Text).

These are then saved as final artwork pages and compiled into the finished book.

Original Text
(The full story)
ISBN:
978-1-906332-17-4

Quick Text
(Fewer words for a fast-paced read)
ISBN:
978-1-906332-18-1

LOOK OUT FOR MORE TITLES
IN THE CLASSICAL COMICS RANGE

Jane Eyre:
The Graphic Novel

Published: 29th September 2008 • 144 Pages • £9.99
• Script Adaptation: Amy Corzine • Artwork: John M. Burns • Letters: Terry Wiley

This Charlotte Brontë classic is brought to vibrant life by artist John M. Burns. His sympathetic treatment of Jane Eyre's life during the 19th century will delight any reader, with its strong emotions and wonderfully rich atmosphere. Travel back to a time of grand mansions contrasted with the severest poverty, and immerse yourself in this fabulous love story.

ISBN: 978-1-906332-06-8

ISBN: 978-1-906332-08-2

Frankenstein:
The Graphic Novel

Published: 29th September 2008 • 144 Pages • £9.99
• Script Adaptation: Jason Cobley • Linework: Declan Shalvey
• Colours: Jason Cardy & Kat Nicholson • Art Direction: Jon Haward • Letters: Terry Wiley

True to the original novel (rather than the square-headed Boris Karloff image from the films!) Declan's naturally gothic artistic style is a perfect match for this epic tale. Frankenstein is such a well known title; yet the films strayed so far beyond the original novel that many people today don't realise how this classic horror tale deals with such timeless subjects as alienation, empathy and understanding beyond appearance. Another great story, beautifully crafted into a superb graphic novel.

ISBN: 978-1-906332-15-0

ISBN: 978-1-906332-16-7

OTHER CLASSICAL COMICS TITLES:

Great Expectations
Published: January 2009
Original Text   978-1-906332-09-9
Quick Text   978-1-906332-11-2

Romeo & Juliet
Published: July 2009
Original Text   978-1-906332-19-8
Plain Text   978-1-906332-20-4
Quick Text   978-1-906332-21-1

Richard III
Published: March 2009
Original Text   978-1-906332-22-8
Plain Text   978-1-906332-23-5
Quick Text   978-1-906332-24-2

Dracula
Published: September 2009
Original Text   978-1-906332-25-9
Quick Text   978-1-906332-26-6

The Tempest
Published: May 2009
Original Text   978-1-906332-29-7
Plain Text   978-1-906332-30-3
Quick Text   978-1-906332-31-0

The Canterville Ghost
Published: October 2009
Original Text   978-1-906332-27-3
Quick Text   978-1-906332-28-0

For more information visit www.classicalcomics.com

TEACHERS' RESOURCES

To accompany each title in our series of graphic novels, we also publish a set of teachers' resources. These widely acclaimed photocopiable books are designed by teachers, for teachers, to help them meet the requirements of the UK curriculum guidelines. Aimed at upper Key Stage 2 and above, each book provides exercises that cover structure, listening, understanding, motivation and comprehension as well as key words, themes and literary techniques. Although the majority of the tasks focus on the use of language in order to align with the revised framework for teaching English, you will also find many cross-curriculum topics, covering areas within history, ICT, drama, reading, speaking, writing and art; and with a range of skill levels, they provide many opportunities for differentiated teaching and the tailoring of lessons to meet individual needs.

Classical Comics Study Guide: A Christmas Carol

Black and white, spiral bound A4 making it easy to photocopy.

Price: £19.99
ISBN: 978-1-906332-38-9
Published: October 2008

DIFFERENTIATED TEACHING AT YOUR FINGERTIPS!

"Because the exercises feature illustrations from the graphic novel, they provide an immediate link for students between the book and the exercise – however they can also be used in conjunction with any traditional text; and many of the activities can be used completely stand-alone. I think the guide is fantastic and I look forward to using it. I know it will be a great help and lead to engaging lessons . It is easy to use, another major asset. Seriously: well done, well done, well done!"

Kornel Kossuth,
Head of English, Head of General Studies

"Thank you! These will be fantastic for all our students. It is a brilliant resource and to have the lesson ideas too are great. Thanks again to all your team who have created these."
B.P. KS3

"Thank you so much. I can't tell you what a help it will be."
A very grateful teacher, Kerryann SA

"...you've certainly got a corner of East Anglia convinced that this is a fantastic way to teach and progress English literature and language!!"
Chris Mehew

"With many thanks again for your excellent resources and upbeat philosophy."
Dr. Marcella McCarthy,
Leading Teacher for Gifted and Talented Education,
The Cherwell School, Oxford

"Dear Classical Comics,
Can I just say a quick "thank you" for the excellent teachers' resources that accompanied the *Henry V* Classical Comics. I needed to look no further for ideas to stimulate my class. The children responded with such enthusiasm to the different formats for worksheets, it kept their interest and I was able to find appropriate challenges for all abilities. The book itself was read avidly by even the most reluctant readers. Well done, I'm looking forward to seeing the new titles."
A. Dawes, Tockington Manor School

"I wanted to write to thank you - I had a bottom set Y9 class that would have really struggled with the text if it wasn't for your comics, THANK YOU."
Dan Woodhouse

"As to the resource, I can't wait to start using it! Well done on a fantastic service."
Will

OUR RANGE OF OTHER CLASSICAL COMICS STUDY GUIDES

Henry V	Macbeth	Jane Eyre	Frankenstein	Great Expectations
Published: November 2007	Published: March 2008	Published: October 2008	Published: October 2008	Published: January 2009
Price: £19.99	Price: £19.99	Price: £19.99	Price: £19.99	Price: £19.99
ISBN: 978-1-906332-07-5	ISBN: 978-1-906332-10-5	ISBN: 978-1-906332-12-9	ISBN: 978-1-906332-37-2	ISBN: 978-1-906332-13-6

BRINGING CLASSICS TO COMIC LIFE

Classical Comics has partnered with Comic Life to bring you a unique comic creation experience!

Comic Life is an award-winning software system that is used and loved by millions of children, adults and schools around the world. The software allows you to create astounding comics in a matter of minutes – and it is really easy and fun to use, too!

Through RM Distribution, you can now obtain all of our titles in every text version, electronically for use with any computer or whiteboard system. In addition, you can also obtain our titles as "No Text" versions that feature just the beautiful artwork without any speech bubbles or captions. These files can then be used in Comic Life (or any other

software that can handle jpg files) enabling anyone to create their own version of one of our famous titles.

All of the digital versions of our titles are available from RM on a single user or site-license basis.

For more details, visit www.rm.com and search for Classical Comics, or visit www.classicalcomics.com / education.

Classical Comics, RM and Comic Life - Bringing Classics to Comic Life!

OUT NOW AND AVAILABLE
FROM ALL GOOD BOOKSHOPS

OUR SHAKESPEARE TITLES ARE AVAILABLE IN THREE TEXT FORMATS

Each text version uses the same exquisite full-colour artwork providing a completely flexible reading experience: - you simply choose which version is right for you!

Original Text — THE UNABRIDGED ORIGINAL PLAY BROUGHT TO LIFE IN FULL COLOUR!

Plain Text — THE COMPLETE PLAY TRANSLATED INTO PLAIN ENGLISH!

Quick Text — THE FULL PLAY IN QUICK MODERN ENGLISH FOR A FAST-PACED READ!

Henry V: The Graphic Novel

Published: 5th November 2007 • 144 Pages • £9.99
• Script Adaptation: John McDonald • Pencils: Neill Cameron • Inks: Bambos • Colours: Jason Cardy & Kat Nicholson • Letters: Nigel Dobbyn

Macbeth: The Graphic Novel

Published: 25th February 2008 • 144 Pages • £9.99
• Script Adaptation: John McDonald • Pencils: & Inks: Jon Haward • Inking Assistant: Gary Erskine • Colours & Letters: Nigel Dobbyn

ISBN: 978-1-906332-00-6

ISBN: 978-1-906332-01-3

ISBN: 978-1-906332-02-0

ISBN: 978-1-906332-03-7

ISBN: 978-1-906332-04-4

ISBN: 978-1-906332-05-1